Adventures

#3

WHO'S SAYING NASTY THINGS ABOUT ME... ONLINE?!

Monica

Monica is a sweet, happy, buck-toothed, teenage girl. When she was younger, she was known for being intolerant of disrespect and always stood up for her friends. That is, unless Jimmy-Five and Smudge would cause her trouble, then Monica would bash them with her favorite plush blue bunny, Samson! Still, occasionally, she does her classic bunny bashings as a teen, but has chilled out when it comes to Jimmy-Five, who has been catching her attention a lot more lately. Monica is the leader of the gang because of her honest and charismatic—and powerful—personality.

J-Five

Jimmy-Five, or J-Five, has always been picked on for his speech impediment. He used to lisp, which caused him to switch letters around, such as r's for w's, when he would speak. He has grown out of that as a teen, unless he's nervous, which typically happens around a certain girl. He also was picked on because of the five strands of hair he had on his head, which have all sort of filled out as a teen. Still, J-Five is sometimes made fun of for his hair, but he doesn't let it get to him as much anymore! When J-Five was young, he would often try to steal Monica's blue bunny from her and attempt to take over as leader of the gang with his questionable schemes. J-Five is no longer focused on being head of the gang as much as he's focused on being close with his friends, and closer to one friend in particular...

Smudge

Smudge has never liked water and prefers his messy and dirty lifestyle over showers, rain, swimming, or even drinking water any day, but he's warmed up to taking showers as a teen… sort of. He cleans up sometimes mainly because the opinion of girls has started to matter to him, unlike when he was a kid. Smudge loves sports, especially skateboarding and soccer because of how radical they are. He also loves comics, and shares this love with his best friend, J-Five! Smudge is kind of the "handyman" of the gang, always helping his friends in times of need but typically also messing everything up.

Maggy

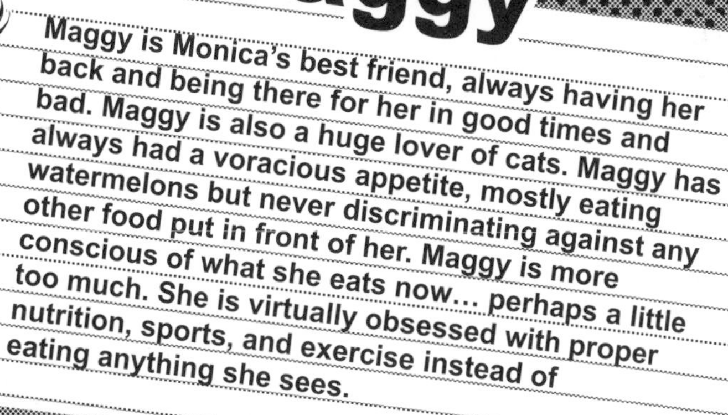

Maggy is Monica's best friend, always having her back and being there for her in good times and bad. Maggy is also a huge lover of cats. Maggy has always had a voracious appetite, mostly eating watermelons but never discriminating against any other food put in front of her. Maggy is more conscious of what she eats now… perhaps a little too much. She is virtually obsessed with proper nutrition, sports, and exercise instead of eating anything she sees.

#3 "Who's Saying Nasty Things About Me...Online?!"

Characters, Story, and Illustration created by MAURICIO DE SOUSA
ZAZO AGUIAR and WELLINGTON DIAS—Cover Artists
PETRA LEÃO—Script
MARCELO CASSARO and LINO PAES—Pencils
CAROLINE HONDA, CRISTINA H. ANDO, JAIME PODAVIN, PAULO ROBERTO MATHEUS COSTA, RONASA G. VALIM, and TATIANA MONTEIRO—Inks
MARCELO CASSARO—Lettering
MARIA DE FÁTIMA A. CLARO, MARIA APARECIDA RABELLO, and JAE HYUNG WOO—Art Coordination
MAURICIO DE SOUSA, MARINA TAKEDA E SOUSA—Script Supervisors
ALICE K. TAKEDA—Executive Director
SIDNEY GUSMAN—Editorial Planner
WAGNER BONILLA—Art Director
ÍVANA MELLO, SOLANGE M. LEMES—Original editors
PECCAVI TRANSLATIONS—Original Translations
Special thanks to LOURDES GALIANO, GRACIELE PEREIRA, RODRIGO PAIVA, TATIANE COMLOSI, MARINA TAKEDA E SOUSA, MÔNICA SOUSA, and MAURICO DE SOUSA

JEFF WHITMAN—Editor, Production, Dialog Restoration
KARR ANTUNES—Editorial Intern
JIM SALICRUP
Editor-in-Chief

Charmz is an imprint of Papercutz.

PB ISBN: 978-1-5458-0325-7
HC ISBN: 978-1-5458-0324-0

Printed in China
July 2019

Charmz books may be purchased for business or promotional use.
For information on bulk purchases please contact Macmillan
Corporate and Premium Sales Department at
(800) 221-7945 x5442

Distributed by Macmillan
First Charmz Printing

...IS TO GET AN UNDERSTANDING OF "INFORMATION"...

COMPUTER LAB

TRY TO IMAGINE, JUST A FEW YEARS AGO...
...YOU'D HAVE TO LOOK IN MANUALS, BOOKS, MAPS, ALMANACS, ENCYCLOPEDIAS, AND/OR MAGAZINES TO FIND INFORMATION!

TODAY, ALL THAT INFORMATION IS AT YOUR FINGERTIPS WITH JUST A SIMPLE "CLICK"!

HUH?

DENISE SAYS: WANT SOME JUICY GOSSIP? >>
CLICKHERE.CLICKHERE.CLIC

OBTAINING INFORMATION IS A LOT FASTER NOW...
HEE-HEE... HEE-HEE...
HEE-HEE... HEE-HEE...
HA-HA...

...WITH FASTER INTERNET ACCESS AND ONLINE INTERACTION AND COLLABORATION...
HA-HA! HA-HA!
HEE-HEE! HEE-HEE!
HEE-HEE-HEE!
SNORT!
HA-HA-HA-HA!
BWHA-HA-HA!
HEE-HEE-HEE!

HA-HA-HA!
HA-HA-HA!
HA-HA-HA!
HAAAAA...!

WOULD YOU LIKE TO TELL ME WHAT'S SO FUNNY, TONY?

NOTHING AT ALL, MRS. M.!
I'M LOVIN' ALL THIS TALK ABOUT INFO AND INTERACTION AND ALL THAT...

PFFFT... PFF... HEH...

AHAHAHAHAHAHAHAH AHAHAHAHAHAHAHAHA HAHAHAHAHAHAHAHAH AHAHAHAHAHAHAHAHA
SMUDGE!
YOU WON'T BE LAUGHING...
...WHEN I TAKE POINTS OFF YOUR FINAL GRADE!
GULP!
M-MY BAD, MRS. MONTGOMERY! IT'S NOT MY FAULT, THOUGH.

DENISE WAS BUSY SENDING ME FUNNY THINGS OVER MESSENGER, AND I--
AAHHH! SNITCH! TWO-FACE! VENOMOUS SNAKE!

IS THIS TRUE, DENISE?
ARE YOU PASSING NOTES DURING CLASS?

GET REAL, TEACH! CHAT IS INSTALLED ON **EVERY** MACHINE.

WHAT DID YOU EXPECT US TO ONLY SHARE CHEMISTRY FORMULAS WITH ONE ANOTHER?
WHAT I WANT TO KNOW IS...

...WHAT IS **SO IMPORTANT** THAT YOU NEEDED TO SHARE WITH THE WHOLE CLASS IN SECRET?

OHHH, CHECK OUT THE *TEACH*!
WHAT YOU MEAN TO SAY IS YOU'RE JUST **DYING** TO KNOW AS WELL?

B-BUT... YEAH... OOPS.

I WAS JUST DEMONSTRATING THE POWER OF THIS MEGA-MAGICAL MODERN INFORMATION SHARER.
IT'S RIDICULOUSLY FAST...

...NOW, WE ALL KNOW A LITTLE SOMETHING MORE ABOUT ONE OF OUR FRIENDS.

WHAT IN THE WORLD IS THAT?!
GREAT QUESTION! WHAT IS IT, SUNNY?
IT'S SO FOOLISH, I DON'T EVEN GET IT.
A-A P-PICTURE OF ME? B-BUT H-HOW?!

Troll Castle
The Sum of All Things Troll
"TROLL CASTLE"? WHAT IS THIS SITE?

IT JUST LOOKS LIKE A BLOG WITH PICTURES AND GOSSIP!
"JUST"? THIS IS THE BEST THING EVER!

"TROLL CASTLE" IS THE HOTTEST, GO-TO PLACE FOR ALL THINGS RELATING TO NEIGHBORHOOD INFORMATION.
IT CONTAINS EVERYTHING THAT IS **IN**, HAS BEEN **IN**, AND WILL BE **IN**!

A SITE JUST FOR TRASH TALKING OTHER STUDENTS?
WHAT A WASTE OF TIME!
DON'T MAKE IT OUT TO BE A SMALL THING, **MARINA**! IT'S SO MUCH **MORE** THAN THAT!
DEEP, DARK SECRETS! BAD TIPPERS! UNBELIEVABLE DISH!
IT'S A TREASURE CHEST FILLED WITH TONS OF SCOOPS, TEA, AND BLIND ITEMS!
I READ IT **EVERY DAY**! **ALL. DAY. LONG.**

CASTLE? I THOUGHT TROLLS LIVED IN CAVES.
AT LEAST THAT'S WHAT FAIRY TALES TELL US.
RPG GAMES TOO!

RIGHT. A TROLL IS A MONSTER FROM NORSE MYTHOLOGY...

...BUT THAT, THAT'S A TOTALLY DIFFERENT TROLL.
A TROLL ON THE INTERNET IS SOMEONE WHO ONLY SAYS THINGS TO MESS WITH OTHERS.
WHAT DO YOU MEAN?

A **TROLL** WILL FIND A WAY TO INJECT THEMSELVES INTO ANY CONVERSATION JUST TO DERAIL IT.

A *TROLL* GOES INTO **BLOGS,** SOCIAL MEDIA, AND ANY PLACE THEY CAN LEAVE A COMMENT ONLINE...
...AND STARTS CURSING, FIGHTING, AND ENRAGING OTHERS UNTIL EVERYONE LOSES THEIR PATIENCE.

YOU DON'T UNDERSTAND ANYTHING ABOUT GLOBAL TRENDS, THE MARKET IS GOING THROUGH A CRISIS.

I FEEL TARGETED AND TRIGGERED RIGHT NOW. YOU ARE OFFENDING ME, I'M NOT GOING TO RESPOND TO THAT.

YOU'RE JUST HERE TO CREATE CONFUSION. I'M DONE WITH THIS CONVERSATION.

SERIOUSLY? SO, WHEN YOU WERE YOUNGER, **J-FIVE**...
...**YOU** WERE KIND OF A *TROLL*?

HUMPH NOT AT ALL.
BECAUSE A **REAL** *TROLL* IS A **COWARD**.

A TROLL SAYS ALL THE THINGS ONLINE THEY WOULD NEVER SAY IN PERSON.
THEY USE THE INTERNET TO IRRITATE EVERYONE BECAUSE THEY THINK THEY ARE SAFE FROM DETECTION.

AND I ALWAYS TEASED YOU, MONICA, TO YOUR FACE.
EVEN WHEN I WAS AT RISK OF GETTING HIT OVER THE HEAD BY YOUR PLUSH RABBIT.
YEAH... I CAN'T ARGUE WITH THAT.
STILL... YOU WERE A HUGE PEST.

AND THERE'S A WHOLE BUNCH OF WAYS TO TROLL PEOPLE.
LIKE SPREADING CONTROVERSIAL "FAKE NEWS."

...JUST TO SEE HOW PEOPLE REACT.
WHOA! IS THIS FOR REAL?

SO, **DUSTINE** USES HYDROGEN PEROXIDE IN HER HAIR?
HEY!

THAT IS AN ABSOLUTE INVASION OF PRIVACY, THAT'S WHAT THAT IS!

JUST LIKE ANY OTHER GREAT INVENTION BY HUMANKIND, THE INTERNET BRINGS GREAT THINGS...
... BUT ALSO, SOME **DANGEROUS THINGS**.

AND THIS IS ONE OF THOSE THINGS.
TOO MUCH EXPOSURE OF INTIMATE DETAILS OVER SOCIAL MEDIA.

UGH! WHEN YOU SAY IT LIKE THAT, YOU TAKE ALL THE FUN OUT OF GOSSIP...
SUNNY HAD A PRIVATE PHOTO EXPOSED BY AN **ANONYMOUS** SOURCE...

DOESN'T ANYONE CARE HOW YOUR VERY OWN FRIEND FEELS ABOUT THIS?
...JUST SO THAT OTHERS CAN LAUGH.

WELL... I...

...I THOUGHT IT WAS THE **COOLEST** THING!
NO ONE **EVER** TALKS ABOUT ME!

OH, WOW. KIDS THESE DAYS
DON'T BE THAT WAY, TEACH!

Old coach learns
fling, M
YOU'RE NOT LEFT OUT...

Old coach learns new tricks, leaving his fling, Mrs. Montgomery, out to d
OR MAYBE **YOU ARE,** KINDA?

CLASS IS OUT EARLY, I GUESS. SEE THAT?
SEE HOW **ESSENTIAL** THESE **SITES** ARE?

ESSENTIAL, YEAH...

... FOR THOSE THAT LIKE MEDDLING IN OTHER PEOPLE'S LIVES.
FINE, *HUN*! ACT LIKE A SAINT ALL YOU WANT, OKAY?

I **SAW** YOU **LIKE** THAT POST FROM YOUR PHONE!
U-UM... IT'S JUST... WELL...

LET'S GET ONE THING STRAIGHT, OKAY?
EVEN MO' GIGGLED A BIT.

SHE'S TOTALLY ALL ABOUT THE DRAMA... IT'S TYPICAL BAGGAGE OF BEING A PRINCIPAL CHARACTER.
WELL, I...
WAIT A MINUTE! WHAT DO YOU MEAN?!

I'M JUST SAYING THAT THERE IS NOWHERE TO HIDE, *PUMPKIN*!

YA'LL CAN PRETEND AS MUCH AS YOU'D LIKE...
...BUT THE WORLD REVOLVES AROUND SOME JUICY GOSSIP!

RIGHT! I HAVE TO ADMIT, IT REALLY WAS FUNNY...

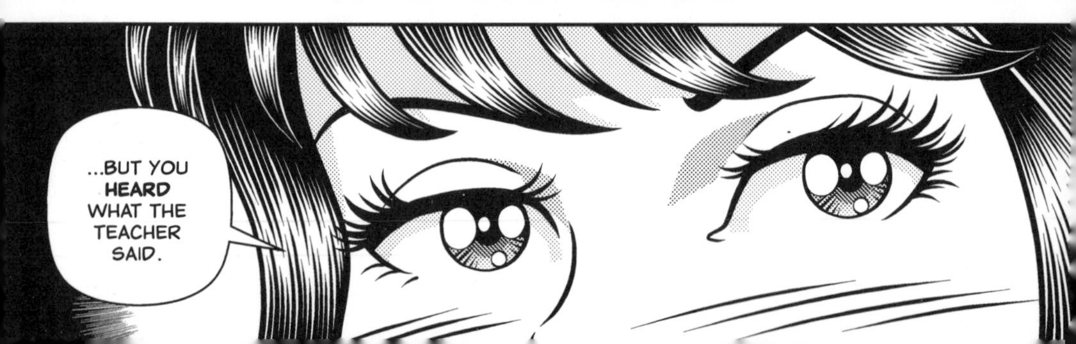
...BUT YOU **HEARD** WHAT THE TEACHER SAID.

THIS TYPE OF INFORMATION IS AN **INVASION OF PRIVACY.**
"PRIVACY"? IS THAT STILL A THING, NOWADAYS?

IT DOESN'T EXIST AT ALL!

WITH THE WORLD FULL OF CAMERAS AND WIFI...

...KEEPING **ANYTHING** SECRET BECOMES MORE AND MORE DIFFICULT.

AND ALL OF IT BECAUSE OF PEOPLE LIKE **YOU**!
OH, FOR CRYING OUT LOUD! SPARE ME.

HELLO! GET A CLUE!
WHO DOESN'T LIKE CALLING ATTENTION TO THEMSELVES?

LOOK AT SUNNY. THAT SELF-SATISFIED FACE IS PROOF ENOUGH.

IT'S TRUE! HE'S **LOVING** BEING NOTICED FOR A CHANGE.
WHO KNOWS? MAYBE HE SENT THE PICTURE TO THE BLOG **HIMSELF**.

WHAT IS IT THAT PEOPLE SAY?
THERE'S NO SUCH THING AS BAD PRESS.

NON-SENSE!
I, FOR ONE, DON'T WANT THAT KIND OF EXPOSURE.

I PREFER TO BE A **DIRECTOR** WHO RUNS THINGS BEHIND THE SCENES...
... INSTEAD OF BEING AN ACTOR, THAT EVERYONE LAUGHS AT.

WELL, IF I WERE YOU... I'D PREPARE MYSELF, CUTIE!
SOONER OR LATER, EVERYONE TRIPS UP!

AND WHEN THAT HAPPENS...
... THE **TROLL KING** WILL BE THERE TO DOCUMENT THE MOMENT!

HMPH! NOT WITH ME.
YOU CAN BE SURE OF IT.

LATER, MISTER SOFTIE!

DON'T FORGET TO HUG THAT TOAD, ALRIGHT?
HE'S **GOING TO** HUG THAT THING NO MATTER WHAT. NO NEED TO TELL HIM!

WOW! SUNNY IS CLEARLY BEING MOCKED...

...AND STILL, HE LOOKS HAPPIER THAN EVER.

AND THOSE TWO... HEE-HEE...

SERIOUSLY, DUSTINE! HOW LONG HAVE WE BEEN TOGETHER?

HOW IS IT THAT I ONLY FOUND OUT TODAY YOU BLEACH YOUR HAIR?
I DON'T WANT TO TALK ABOUT THIS!

IF IT'S GOT TO DO WITH WASHING, I'M ALL EARS!

IT REALLY DOES SEEM LIKE IT'S DIFFICULT TO HIDE SOMETHING THESE DAYS.

IT'S GOOD THAT HAIR TRICKS AND STUFFED ANIMALS AREN'T **TERRIBLE SECRETS.**
AND EVERYONE KNOWS ALL ABOUT **SAMSON** ALREADY...

Troll Castle

I MEAN, IT'S JUST A SILLY SITE! IT MAKES PEOPLE LAUGH.
WHAT'S WRONG WITH SOMETHING LIKE THAT?

MAYBE DENISE IS RIGHT.
WE SHOULD WORRY LESS AND HAVE A LITTLE MORE FUN.

HA-HA! SO, APPARENTLY, SUNNY'S SISTER, CHERYL, HAS TO GO TO SUMMER SCHOOL BECAUSE SHE FAILED FIVE CLASSES?
SLANDER!

8:24 PM

CLICK

CLICK

CLICK

I CAN'T BELIEVE **ANDERSON** COULD DO SUCH A THING, **RYAN**!

I DON'T EVEN KNOW WHAT TO SAY, **ANNA**.
HE'S A COLLEAGUE AND A FRIEND OF MINE.
I WOULD NEVER HAVE EXPECTED THIS FROM HIM.

NEITHER WOULD I! BUT THE WORST THING IS...
...FINDING OUT **THIS WAY**.

FROM SOME **ANONYMOUS** SOURCE. **PUBLICLY**. ON THE INTERNET.
PEOPLE I'VE NEVER MET BEFORE KNEW ALL ABOUT ME.

...AND I... I...

TRY AND SEE THE POSITIVE SIDE.
AT LEAST NOW, YOU KNOW THE TRUTH.

YES! BUT AT WHAT COST WILL--

RYAN? WHAT IS IT?
I DON'T KNOW...

I HAVE A FEELING WE'RE BEING WATCHED.

MAYBE I JUST IMAGINED IT...

NOW, THAT'S ENOUGH WASTING TIME WITH SUCH NONSENSE.
TIME TO GET THINGS DONE.

HMMPH! ME? GET TAKEN DOWN BY SOMEONE LIKE THE "KING OF TROLLS"?
YEAH, RIGHT! I DON'T THINK SO!

GOSSIP SITES?! PEOPLE HAVE WAY TOO MUCH TIME ON THEIR HANDS.
HOW CAN ANYONE ENJOY SOMETHING LIKE THAT?!

HEH-HEH! THAT SITE IS SO FUNNY!
IT'S BEEN A WHILE SINCE I'VE LAUGHED THAT HARD!

HMM... "TROLL CASTLE"...
ANOTHER QUICK PEEK WON'T HURT ANYONE.

WHAT IF HE PUT SOMETHING ON THERE ABOUT ME?
I BETTER JUST MAKE SURE...

YUCK! I WONDER WHO HE'S DEFAMING NOW?

LET'S SEE IF ANY NEW POSTS ARE UP.

OOOOHHHH!

HAHAHAHAHAHAHAHAHA! I LOOOVE IT!

BLAH, BLAH, BLAH, BLAH, BLAH, BLAH, BLAH, BLA
TICK TICK TICK CLICK CLICK CLICK CLICK CLICK
BLAH, BLAH, BLAH, BLAH, BLAH, BLAH, BLAH

HEY, GUYS! WHAT'S ALL THIS COMMOTION ABOUT?

MAGGY?! YOU... CAME TODAY?

HUH? WHY WOULDN'T I COME?
I'M NOT SICK OR ANYTHING LIKE THAT.
WELL, I JUST DIDN'T THINK...
...I DIDN'T THINK YOU'D HAVE THE **COURAGE** TO COME.

"COURAGE"? COURAGE FOR WHAT?

OH, MY GOSH!
MONICA! SHE STILL **DOESN'T KNOW**!

MAGS! PLEASE DON'T TELL ME THAT...
...YOU DIDN'T CHECK "**TROLL CASTLE**" THIS MORNING.

UH... NO! AFTER DENISE GOT ON MY CASE...

...I THOUGHT IT WOULD BE BEST TO DELETE IT OFF MY PHONE.
I MEAN USING THAT KIND OF THING FOR ENTER-TAINMENT IS WRONG.
THAT'S A VERY NOBLE APPROACH, GIRLFRIEND.

BUT YOU DIDN'T SEEM TOO WORRIED ABOUT RIGHT AND WRONG...

...WHEN YOU FOLLOWED OUR BIOLOGY TEACHER YESTERDAY.

OH, NO...

MAGGY! I TRIED TO WARN YOU...

...BUT YOU WEREN'T HOME AND YOUR PHONE WAS TURNED OFF.
POOR THING. SHE MUST HAVE FORGOTTEN TO TURN HER PHONE BACK ON...

...AFTER STALKING MR. RUBENS UP AND DOWN THE NEIGHBOR-HOOD.

DON'T SAY THAT! IT'S ALL VERY NATURAL!
OF COURSE, OUR MAGGY WOULD FORGET EVERYTHING...

HAHAHAHAHAHAHAHAHAHAHAHAH
AHAHAHAHAHAHAHAHAHAHAHAHAH
...AFTER SEEING THE RECENTLY SINGLE TEACHER SHE HAS A VIRTUAL CRUSH ON!

KNOCK IT OFF!

I-I H-HAVE ALWAYS ADMIRED MR. RUBENS.

ALL OF YOU KNOW THAT! EVEN TOD KNOWS THAT.
HE AND I HAVE TALKED ALL ABOUT IT VERY SERIOUSLY.
LUCKY, HUH?
NOT EVERYONE WOULD BE COOL WITH THAT MUCH ADMIRATION.

AND YEAH, I JUST STOPPED FOR A LITTLE BIT TO... JUST... JUST **LOOK AT** HIM.

I DON'T HAVE ANYTHING TO HIDE. EVERYONE ALREADY KNOWS ALL THAT.
ALMOST EVERYONE, CUTIE!

ONE PERSON HAD NO IDEA...
... BUT NOW HE DOES!

MAGGY... I NEED YOU TO COME WITH ME.
WE NEED TO HAVE A DISCUSSION IN THE PRINCIPAL'S OFFICE.

WELL, WILL YOU LOOK AT THAT.
EVEN MR. RUBENS READS "TROLL CASTLE."

DIDN'T I TELL YOU THAT EVERYONE LIKES GOSSIP?

CLASS 14-B

YOU WERE RIGHT, DENISE.

YOU KNOW, IF YOU TWO ARE ACTING LIKE THIS, ALL SKETCHY ABOUT THIS WHOLE THING...

...I CAN ONLY IMAGINE WHAT SECRETS THAT **YOU TWO** HAVE TO HIDE!

I DON'T HAVE A **SINGLE** THING TO HIDE, DENISE.
MY LIFE IS AN OPEN BOOK.

AN OPEN BOOK, HUH?
FROM WHAT I HEAR, THERE'S A LOT OF BOOKS OUT THERE...

...WITH A LOT TO READ **BETWEEN THE LINES**!

HUMPH
I HAVE ABSOLUTELY NOTHING TO BE AFRAID OF.
SHE'S NOT LIKE YOU, TONY.

THE WAY YOU'RE ALWAYS UP TO NO GOOD...
...I'M SURPRISED YOU'RE NOT FEATURED ON "TROLL CASTLE" EVERY SINGLE DAY.

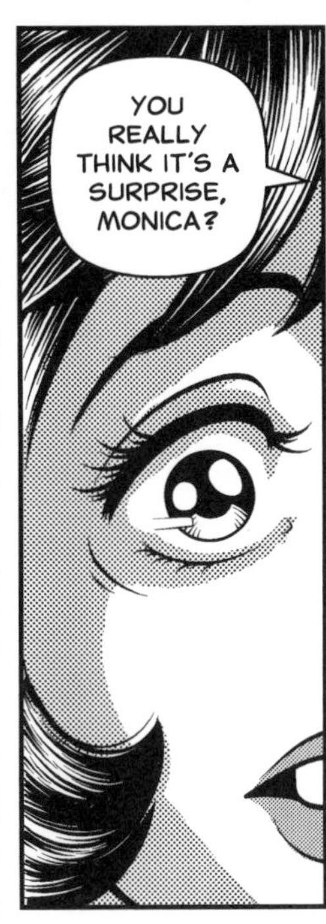
YOU REALLY THINK IT'S A SURPRISE, MONICA?

HA! YOU TWO ARE REAL DENSE.

WHAT DO YOU MEAN?
SERIOUSLY, DON'T YOU GET IT?
MY BAD REPUTATION IS MY GUARANTEED SECURITY.

WHO WOULD WANT TO WASTE TIME **DEFAMING** SOMEONE WHO IS ALREADY **INFAMOUS?**
POINTING OUT THE **OBVIOUS** DOESN'T GET YOU AN AUDIENCE.

WHAT A **SCHMUCK!**
A **SCHMUCK?** ME?

YOU ARE THE ONE THAT IS ALWAYS COMING UP WITH **INFALLIBLE PLANS** BEHIND CLOSED DOORS!
TAKING OVER THE WORLD? THAT'S SO ***CLICHÉ***.
OUCH! LOW BLOW!

I GUARANTEE IT. I'M SAFE FROM THE **KING OF TROLLS.**
HE'S GOT NO WAY OF PUTTING OUT ANY NEWS ON ME.

BUT THE KIDS WHO MAKE THEMSELVES OUT TO BE ***GOODY-TWO-SHOES***...

I N-NEVER...
NEVER IMAGINED THIS COULD HAPPEN.

I'VE NEVER BEEN SO EMBAR-RASSED.
CALM DOWN, MAGGY. IT'S ALL GOING TO BE ALRIGHT.
YOU SAID SO YOURSELF, EVERYONE ALREADY KNEW.

C'MON, MO! HOW CAN I EVER FACE MR. RUBENS NOW?
HE MUST THINK I'M COMPLETELY RIDICULOUS...

HE GAVE ME THE MOTHER OF ALL LECTURES.
TOLD ME THAT SPYING ON PEOPLE WAS **ILLEGAL**!

IMAGINE WHAT HE MUST THINK OF ME RIGHT NOW.
HE MUST THINK I'M SOME KIND OF **DELINQUENT**!
MAGS, TRY AND NOT WORRY SO MUCH ABOUT WHAT...

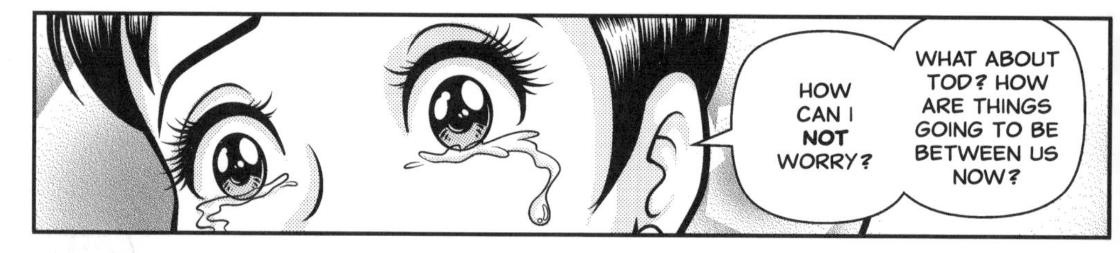
HOW CAN I **NOT** WORRY?
WHAT ABOUT TOD? HOW ARE THINGS GOING TO BE BETWEEN US NOW?

WHEN HE FOUND OUT ABOUT MY... ADMIRATION FOR THE PROFESSOR...
...WE TALKED IT OUT. HE GETS IT.

BUT NOW HE'S GOING TO BE THE LAUGHING STOCK OF HIGH SCHOOL!

HE WON'T RESPOND TO ANY OF MY MESSAGES OR ANSWER ANY OF MY CALLS!
HE MUST HATE ME RIGHT NOW!

AND YOU THINK I SHOULDN'T WORRY?
NO! THAT'S NOT WHAT I MEANT.
I WAS JUST SAYING...

...THAT SOON ENOUGH PEOPLE WILL FORGET ALL ABOUT THIS.

GUYS! DO ANY OF YOU WANT TO MEET "TOADSTER"?
I BROUGHT HIM TO SCHOOL TODAY.
GET REAL, SUNNY. BREAKING NEWS IS HAPPENING!
WHOA! OF ALL PEOPLE, MAGGY?
I DIDN'T KNOW THIS SIDE OF HER...
YESTERDAY, SUNNY WAS THE TARGET OF RIDICULE.
TODAY, IT'S YOU. HE'S OLD NEWS.

TOMORROW, IT'LL BE SOMEONE ELSE.
NO ONE WILL EVEN REMEMBER WHAT HAPPENED TODAY.
SO, I'M ONLY GOING TO HAVE SOME PEACE WHEN THE KING OF TROLLS ATTACKS AGAIN?
THAT DOESN'T SEEM RIGHT...

BESIDES, FRIEND, LET'S AGREE ON ONE THING...
...YOUR INFATUATION WITH RUBENS WAS GETTING A LITTLE OUT OF HAND.

SOMETIMES BAD THINGS HAPPEN FOR GOOD REASONS.
MAYBE THIS WILL ALL HAVE BEEN A BLESSING IN DISGUISE THAT--

RIGHT! I GET IT, NOW!

YOU'RE JUST LIKE THE OTHERS!

HUH?!

YOU **ALSO** THINK THAT I WAS IN THE **WRONG**!
YOU THINK THIS IS MY **FAULT**!

AND THAT I SHOULD BE **HUMILIATED**!

WHAT?! NO!
MAGGY! WAIT!

VERY WELL, MONICA! LET'S JUST WAIT UNTIL YOU TURN UP ON "**TROLL CASTLE**"!
THEN, WE'LL TALK!

I T-THINK I SAID TOO MUCH...

I WAS JUST TRYING TO CHEER MAGGY UP!
THINGS THAT HAPPEN ON THE INTERNET REALLY DO BLOW OVER PRETTY QUICK, THEY--

GET OUT OF MY SIGHT!
I'VE ALREADY TOLD YOU, WE HAVE NOTHING TO TALK ABOUT!
BUT IT'S TRUE! IT WASN'T LIKE THAT! I WAS JUST VISITING MY COUSIN!
COUSIN, TWICE REMOVED... BUT STILL...
HMM... MAYBE NOT THAT QUICK FOR THOSE INVOLVED...

I MEAN... WHY DO PEOPLE GET ALL FREAKED OUT ABOUT THE HONEST TRUTH?
IF J-FIVE WAS HIDING SOMETHING FROM ME...

... I'D WANT TO KNOW. ONE WAY OR ANOTHER.

YOU ARE THE ONE THAT IS FOREVER COMING UP WITH INFALLIBLE PLANS BEHIND CLOSED DOORS!

WHAT IF...?

WHAT IF J-FIVE IS AFRAID THAT I WILL FIND SOMETHING OUT?

1:18 PM
CLICK
CLICK
CLICK
CLICK

EXCELLENT, MARINA!
STUDIO

YOUR ART IS GETTING BETTER EVERY DAY!
DON'T SAY THAT, SIR...

I STILL HAVE A LOT TO IMPROVE ON!
THESE ARE GOING IN THE TRASH...
YES, YES... SEEKING TO CONSTANTLY EVOLVE IS ESSENTIAL...

...BUT DON'T LET HUMILITY CLOUD YOUR CONCEPTS, YOUNG LADY!
THERE IS NOTHING WRONG WITH BEING PROUD OF YOURSELF!

SO MANY AMAZING **PRODUCTIVE** THINGS TO DO WITH OUR TIME...
I DON'T GET HOW PEOPLE PREFER TO **DESTROY** THINGS AS OPPOSED TO **CREATING** THEM!

SPEAKING OF WHICH, AFTER THOSE TECHNOLOGY CLASSES...
... TIME TO PRACTICE A BIT OF **DIGITAL ARTWORK**!

WAIT... WHAT ARE ALL THESE EMAILS?

From: Carmen
SUBJECT: Beautiful Sketches
From: Tony
SUBJECT: Open Book, huh?
From: Denise
SUBJECT: Awkwaaard, Sweetie!

YOU THINK, MAYBE...
NO, NO... IT CAN'T BE!
Troll Castle
NO! NO WAY!

Artsy Artful "Artist" Caught Hiding her Ugly Art to Keep her Perfect Image. Can She Draw a Straight Line?

BUT THOSE **ARE NOT** FINISHED WORKS!
THEY ARE JUST **SKETCHES** THAT DIDN'T WORK!
NO ONE WAS SUPPOSED TO SEE THOSE!

NO ONE SHOULD HAVE SEEN THEM...

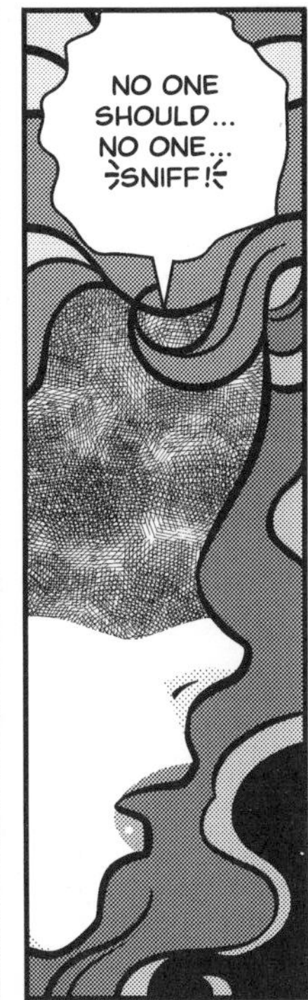
NO ONE SHOULD... NO ONE... SNIFF!

THIS ISN'T FUNNY AT ALL.

THIS IS SERIOUS, IT'S **DANGER-OUS**...
FOR **ALL** OF US.

IT'S NO USE, **IZ**!
I'M SO NERVOUS, I CAN'T EVEN EAT.
MAGGY, PLEASE! EAT SOMETHING.
IT'S RUDE TO WASTE FOOD.

3:34 PM
CLICK

Izzy Double Dips Into her Friend's Grief. Can Maggy Stomach the Shame While Her Friend Steals Her Food?
"IT'S RUDE TO WASTE FOOD," HUH?!
GULP!

BUT, NIMBUS, MAGGY WASN'T GOING TO EAT IT ANYWAY.
IT SHOULDN'T BE MADE OUT TO BE SO WRONG LIKE THAT!
NO! BUT THE WAY THAT THE KING OF TROLLS PRESENTED IT...
...IT LOOKED MORE SERIOUS THAN IT WAS.

4:02 PM
CLICK

Cloudy With a Chance of Meetcute.
Nimbus and Izzy Secret Rendezvous!
Is Love in the Forecast for These Two Teens?
YOU'RE RIGHT, THIS SITE MAKES EVERYTHING LOOK MUCH MORE SERIOUS.

THIS IS ALL WRONG!
I DON'T HAVE A CRUSH ON ANYONE!
N-NO? I, MEAN...
WELL, T-THESE THINGS HAPPEN...

5:15 PM
CLICK

Insensitive Illusionist Breaks Heart of Ramona the Adolescent Witch
MOM?! YOU TOO?
OF COURSE, **RAMONA**! THIS SITE IS ABSOLUTELY **FABULOUS**.
AND THAT'LL TEACH YOU THAT YOU CAN'T TRUST THOSE BOYS.

HBLAHBLAHBLAHBLAHBLAHBLAHBL
HBLAHBLAHBLAHBLAHBLAHBLAHBI

THE TRULY WORST PART IS TO SEE THE **TROLL'S** LATEST **TARGETS**.

MARINA HASN'T DRAWN IN DAYS.
MAGGY ISN'T TALKING TO ME.
NIMBUS HAS BEEN SO DOWN IN THE DUMPS...
HE EVEN STOPPED TALKING TO IZZY. I THINK OUT OF AWK-WARDNESS.

EVEN SUNNY ISN'T HAVING ANY FUN ANYMORE.
IF HE WASN'T TAKEN SERIOUSLY BEFORE, IMAGINE NOW.
GUYS, SERIOUSLY! I NEED SOMEONE TO BE MY LAB PARTNER!
THIS LAB REPORT IS FOR A GRADE!
PARTNER UP WITH YOUR PLUSH FROG, DUDE! HA-HA!

PEOPLE JUST AREN'T THE SAME SINCE ALL OF THIS STARTED.
YEAH! EVERYONE IS TALKING DURING CLASS...

... AND THE TEACHER DOESN'T EVEN CARE.

GRRR! THAT KING OF TROLLS IS HAVING THE TIME OF HIS LIFE!
YEP! THAT'S WHO I WANT TO FOCUS ON.

WHAT DO YOU MEAN?

DON'T YOU FIND IT SUSPICIOUS, MO?
THAT THE KING OF TROLLS ONLY DIGS UP GOSSIP IN THIS NEIGH-BORHOOD?
ALWAYS ABOUT OUR FRIENDS?

IT'S BECAUSE WE ARE IMPORTANT.
THERE, I SAID IT.

HMM... DON'T YOU THINK YOU'RE BEING A LITTLE BIT FULL OF YOURSELF?
IMPORTANT, SMUDGE? US?

SURE, THERE ARE PEOPLE THAT LOVE TO PICK ON CELEB-RITIES ON THE INTERNET...

... BUT THAT'S NOT WHAT WE ARE.
MAYBE NOT TO THE WORLD...

Up and Coming Athlete in Lemon Tree Spends Most of His Time Falling Down
BUT WE ARE CERTAINLY IMPORTANT IN HIS MIND.

AND HE'S TRYING TO PROVE THAT WE'RE NO BIG DEAL.
I'M CERTAIN OF IT.

YOU KNOW WHAT? I THINK SMUDGE MAY BE ON TO SOMETHING.

THAT'S WHY THE KING OF TROLLS WON'T GET OFF OUR BACKS.
SO... HE'S SOMEONE THAT ***KNOWS*** US?

YES! HE KNOWS US...

... AND HE'S **JEALOUS** OF US.

BUT... WHO IS IT?
WHO COULD HAVE SO MUCH ANIMOSITY TOWARDS US?

OH, BOY! YOU WANT A LIST?
VIVIAN THE WITCH, CAPTAIN FRAY, YUKA, ALANDRIA...
THOSE ARE THE OBVIOUS GUESSES...

... BUT I HAVE MY SUSPICIONS THAT IT MIGHT BE SOMEONE FROM **INSIDE** OUR GROUP.
WHAT?! A **TRAITOR?**

THINK ABOUT IT. THIS KING OF TROLLS GOT A PICTURE OF SUNNY **SLEEPING**...
... AND STOLE MARINA'S DRAWINGS THAT SHE THREW AWAY ***HERE*** AT THE SCHOOL.

AND KNEW EXACTLY WHERE TO FIND MAGGY, IZZY, NIMBUS, RAMONA...
I NEVER THOUGHT OF THAT!

EITHER IT'S SOME GUY WITH **NO LIFE...**
... OR SOMEONE THAT ALREADY KNOWS ALL OF OUR DAILY HABITS.
AND KNOWS WHERE WE **LIVE**.

YES! WE HAVE TO CATCH THE TROLL...
... BEFORE IT'S **TOO LATE**.

TOO LATE?
TOO LATE FOR *WHAT*, J?

HUH?! WHAT DO YOU MEAN?

YEAH, EXACTLY! THIS TROLL IS DOING HORRIBLE THINGS AND WHAT NOT...
...BUT WHAT ARE **YOU** SO WORRIED ABOUT?

WHAT ARE YOU TALKING ABOUT, MONICA? ARE YOU **DEFENDING** THIS GUY?

YOU WANT TO KEEP ENJOYING ALL OF HIS **TROLLING?**
OF COURSE NOT! DON'T PLAY DUMB.

I JUST THINK YOUR PARANOIA IS A LITTLE **SUSPICIOUS**.

AREN'T YOU THE ONE GOING ON AND ON ABOUT AN **INVASION OF PRIVACY**?
ARE YOU SCARED THAT THE TROLL WILL REVEAL SOMETHING ABOUT YOU?

IS THERE A CHANCE THAT MAYBE *YOU* HAVE SOMETHING TO HIDE?

OH, **COME ON!**
YOU'D RATHER LET THE TROLL TORMENT THE WHOLE GANG...

... JUST TO SEE IF THERE'S SOMETHING TO FIND OUT ABOUT ME?

I THINK MONICA MIGHT BE ON TO SOMETHING, DUDE...

MY DUDE, IF EVEN MARINA APPEARED ON THE **TROLL CASTLE** SITE...
SMUDGE?!
WHOSE SIDE ARE YOU ON, **FWIEND?**

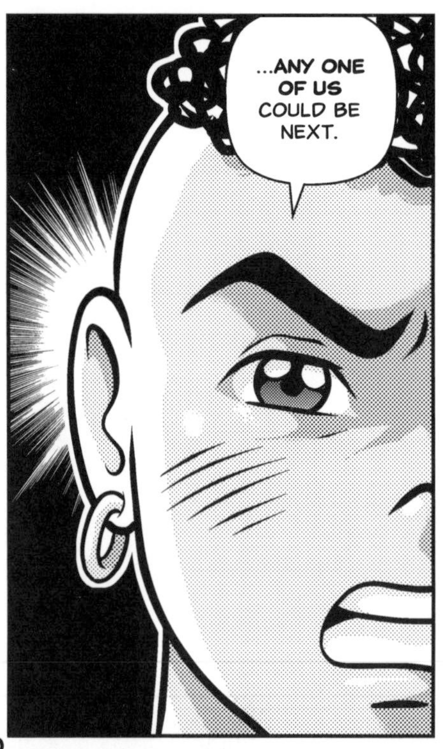
...**ANY ONE OF US** COULD BE NEXT.

THAT'S... THAT'S TRUE FOR **EVERY ONE OF US**!

THAT'S RIGHT...
...EVEN **YOU,** MONICA.

EVERYONE HAS SECRETS.
I BET YOU HAVE SOME TOO.

MAYBE I SHOULD GIVE IN, THOUGH!
LET THIS TROLL KING KEEP TROLLING AS MUCH AS HE WANTS!

JUST SO I CAN SHOW YOU I HAVE NOTHING TO HIDE.

OR TO SHOW HOW WELL YOU'RE CAPA-BLE OF HIDING SOMETHING, YOU MEAN!

UH... GUYS? YOU STILL DON'T GET IT?
IF THE KING OF TROLLS KNOWS ALL OF US...
... THEN THIS IS EXACTLY WHAT HE WANTS.

HE WANT'S EVERYONE TO BE **SCARED**!
TENSE! NERVOUS! PARANOID! UNTRUSTING!

HE'S TRYING TO **DIVIDE** US!

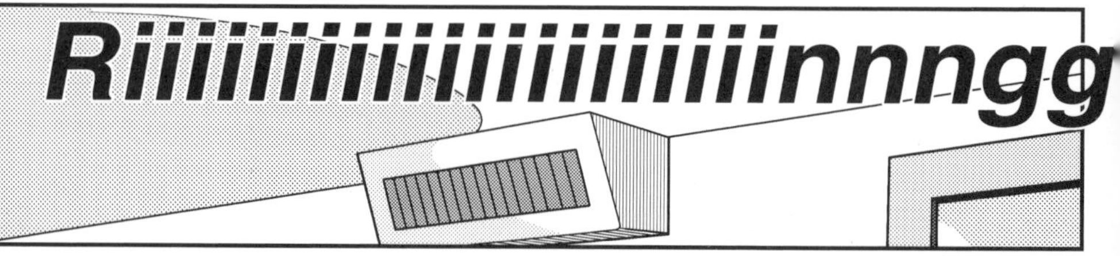
Riiiiiiiiiiiiiiiiiiiinnngg

AND BY THE LOOKS OF IT...
...HE'S ALREADY SUCCEED-ING.

MONICA... ALL WORKED UP, SO AGGRESSIVE...
AH... THE POSSIBILITIES ARE ENDLESS.

AFTER ALL, YOU'VE YET TO HAVE YOUR TURN AT THE **TROLL CASTLE.**
THE MOST POPULAR GIRL IN THE NEIGH-BORHOOD
... DESERVES THE MOST **JAW-DROPPING** POST EVER.

AND I KNOW **EXACTLY** WHAT TO DO.

NO!
I DON'T WANT TO LOOK AT THE INTERNET!

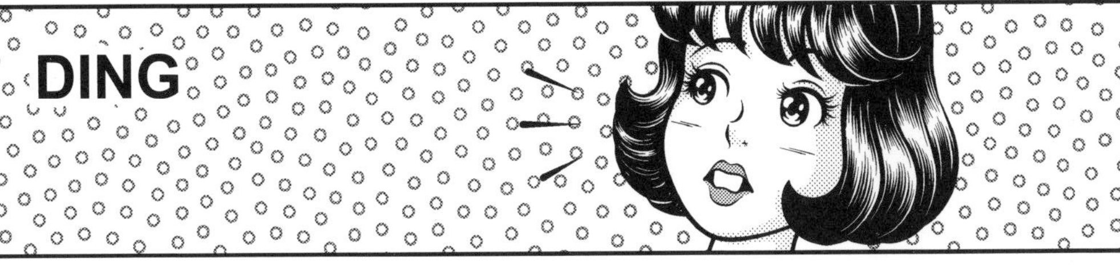
DING

HUH? A TEXT MESSAGE?

Do you wish to receive new notifications from TROLL CASTLE?

GROSS! NO!
I DON'T WANT TO HEAR ONE MORE THING HAVING TO DO WITH THAT SITE!

WELL... HONESTLY, I **WANT** TO...
BUT I KNOW THAT I **SHOULDN'T.**

HOW CAN SOMEONE COMPLETELY ANONYMOUS GET SO MUCH OF MY ATTENTION?
EVEN WITHOUT ME ACCESSING THE SITE... WITHOUT READING A THING...

... I'M STILL FEELING SO **ANXIOUS**.

I KEEP WONDERING IF THE NEXT POST WILL BE ABOUT J-FIVE.

OF COURSE, I WANT TO KNOW EVERYTHING ABOUT HIM, AND...
HE'S IMPORTANT TO ME. I CAN'T HELP IT.

ARGH! I CAN'T GET THESE THOUGHTS OUT OF MY HEAD!

A WALK WOULD CLEAR MY MIND.

I THINK SMUDGE MIGHT HAVE BEEN RIGHT.
THIS WHOLE THING IS DRIVING ALL OF US APART.

IT'S MAKING US DOUBT ONE ANOTHER.
EVEN THOUGH J-FIVE HAS KIND OF ALWAYS CAUSED DOUBT!

MAYBE I'M JUST BEING PARANOID AND...

AND...

I KNEW IT!

I KNEW IT!

LEMON TREE DINER

MONICA?
I KNEW THERE WAS SOMETHING GOING ON BETWEEN YOU AND IRENE!
THAT'S WHAT YOU WERE HIDING FROM ME, ISN'T IT?!

>HMPH!< YOU SHOULD BE ASHAMED OF YOUR-SELF!
I DIDN'T EVEN HAVE TO LOOK ON ***TROLL CASTLE*** TO FIND OUT THAT...

JUST STOP TALKING!
YOU THINK I'M THAT BIG OF AN **IDIOT?**
YOU THINK IF THIS MEET UP WAS A SECRET...
... I'D BE DOING IT IN THE **MOST POPULAR DINER IN THE NEIGH-BORHOOD?**
W-WELL... WHEN YOU PUT IT THAT WAY...

AND YOU'VE GOT ***SOME NERVE*** TO ACCUSE ME...

...AFTER WHAT YOU DID!

BUT...
BUT WHAT
IS...?

DON'T YOU PLAY INNOCENT WITH ME RIGHT NOW!
YOU WERE MAKING A BIG DEAL ABOUT MY SECRETS...

... BUT DIDN'T STOP TO THINK ABOUT YOURS, DID YOU?

BUT...
BUT...

BUT I'VE NEVER SEEN THIS GUY!
I DON'T EVEN KNOW WHO THAT IS!

OH, RIGHT! YOU EXPECT ME TO BELIEVE THAT?

IF IT WAS A PICTURE OF ME KISSING SOMEONE ELSE...
... AND ME SAYING THAT I'D NEVER MET HER...
... YOU'RE TELLING ME YOU'D BELIEVE THAT?

YOU KNOW WHAT? YOU WERE RIGHT!
IT'S A GOOD THING I HAVEN'T UNMASKED THE KING OF TROLLS...

... IT'S THE ONLY WAY SOMEONE WOULD UNMASK YOU!

I DON'T EVER WANT TO SEE YOU AGAIN!

BUT... I...

P-PLEASE! YOU GUYS DON'T BELIEVE THIS, RIGHT?

WOW, THAT'S SOMETHING I DID NOT SEE COMING.
YOU GOT TO ADMIT, IT'S PRETTY SHOCKING STUFF.
YOU THINK YOU KNOW SOMEONE...

CAN'T YOU GUYS SEE WHAT'S HAPPENING?! THIS IS A SET-UP!
THIS PICTURE IS **FAKE**! IT'S EDITED! I DON'T KNOW HOW!

J IS REALLY UPSET, MONICA!
IRENE?

HE CAME TO MEET UP WITH ME HERE, TO **VENT**!

I DON'T KNOW WHY YOU WOULD DO SOME-THING LIKE THAT...
... BUT J-FIVE DIDN'T DESERVE IT!

NOBODY BELIEVES ME. **NOBODY**!

THIS KING OF TROLLS...
IT STARTED WITH PICTURES AND GOSSIP THAT WERE AT LEAST TRUE... IT GOT EVERYONE'S ATTENTION AND TRUST...

... AND THEN CAME THIS BLATANTLY EPIC LIE!

AND EVERYONE FELL FOR IT! EVERYONE... KING OF TROLLS...

I'M COMING FOR YOU!

IT'LL BE TOUGH WITHOUT J-FIVE'S INTELLIGENCE AND COMPUTER SKILLS...
... BUT I'M NO **DUMMY.**

LET'S SEE... THE KING OF TROLLS IS SOMEONE THAT'S KNOWN THE GANG SINCE CHILDHOOD!
SOMEONE THAT IS JEALOUS OF OUR HAPPINESS.

THERE ARE A LOT OF SUSPECTS. IT COULD EVEN BE AN ADULT.
IT COULD EVEN BE MR. BILL!

NO! THE ADULTS THAT WE KNOW ALL HAVE JOBS AND BUSY SCHEDULES.

THE TROLL HAS A LOT OF FREE TIME, ALL THEY DO IS FOLLOW PEOPLE AROUND AND PHOTOGRAPH THEM.

THE NEW POSTS ARE ALWAYS IN THE AFTER-NOON AND AT NIGHT.

THAT MUST MEAN THAT HE'S BUSY IN THE MORNING. LIKE ME.
HE MUST BE A **STUDENT**!

WHO WOULD GO TO ALL THESE LENGTHS JUST TO FABRICATE GOSSIP AND--

HONEY! ONE OF YOUR GIRLFRIENDS IS HERE, WANTING TO TALK TO YOU!
UGH! I DON'T WANT TO SEE **ANYONE**!

TELL HER I'M AWAY ON A **SPIRITUAL RETREAT!**

I D-DON'T THINK SHE'S GOING TO TAKE NO FOR AN ANSWER...
DENISE!
YIKES!
KAPLOW

THERE IS NO POINT IN DENYING ANY OF IT, DENISE! I KNOW EVERYTHING!
SPILL IT! WHY ARE YOU DOING THIS!

I'M SORRY! I'M SORRY! I CONFESS! I CONFESS!
I DON'T KNOW WHAT GOT INTO ME!
PLEASE DON'T HIT ME!

DENISE! HAVE YOU ANY **IDEA** WHAT MAYHEM YOU'VE CAUSED?

I ALWAYS THOUGHT YOU WERE AT LEAST **AUTHENTIC**! **SINCERE**!
BWAAAH! ENOUGH! THERE'S NO NEED TO RUB IT IN!

She Says She's Her True Self But Her Unedited Posts Are Less Than Blemish-Free!
THIS TROLL TOTALLY REVEALED MY SECRET!
NOW, EVERYONE IS GOING TO KNOW I EDIT THE PHOTOS I PUT ONLINE...
... I ERASE ANY BLEMISHES AND REMOVE ANY PIMPLES!

THIS IS THE **THANKS** I GET FOR SHARING AND RE-POSTING THE ***TROLL CASTLE***?
SO... YOU ARE ONE OF HIS VICTIMS AS WELL?

OH, YEAH! YOU WERE ON THERE TODAY!
THAT WAS QUITE THE SHOCKER! LUCKY FOR ME **YOUR** NEWS TOTALLY KNOCKS MINE OUT OF THE WATER!
ARGH! YEAH, ***LUCKY*** YOU!

RIDICULOUS! I WAS SO SURE THAT IT WAS DENISE.
NO ONE LIKED THAT **BLOG** MORE THAN HER.

BUT I HAVE ANOTHER STRONG SUSPECT.

CARMEN! I NEED TO HAVE A WORD WITH YOU...
FASHION

YOU DON'T EVEN HAVE TO SAY ANYTHING. I ALREADY KNOW WHAT IT'S ABOUT.
AND I DON'T OWE AN EXPLANATION TO ANYONE.
DO YOU KNOW HOW SERIOUS THIS IS, MISSY?!

BAH! YOU THINK YOU CAN THREATEN ME?
MY REPUTATION ALREADY WENT DOWN THE DRAIN. IT CAN'T GET ANY WORSE THAN THAT!
LEAVE ME ALONE! I HAVE TO FIND REPLACEMENTS FOR MY ENTIRE WARDROBE.
Dresses Better Than You, Richer Than You, But Still Uses Knock-Off Clothing. We Have the Proof!
Deoore
Deoore

WELL, TO BE FAIR, EVERY-ONE KNOWS **THAT BRAND** SHOULDN'T HAVE SO MANY LETTERS
EXCUSE ME, NO ONE ASKED YOUR OPINION, MISS!

YOU! YOU ARE THE KING OF TROLLS!
IT CAN ONLY BE YOU BEHIND THIS WHOLE THING!

M-MONICA! THAT HURTS! ME?!

I WAS A VICTIM OF THE SITE TOO, REMEMBER?

I KNOW, BUT...

EVERYONE IN THIS NEIGHBORHOOD HAS APPEARED ON THE TROLL CASTLE!
NOT A SINGLE PERSON WAS LEFT OUT!

AND EVERYONE GOT HURT BY THEIR POSTS...
...YOU'RE THE ONLY ONE THAT WAS HAPPY!

YOU HAVE THE MOST REASONS TO BE JEALOUS!
AS A SECONDARY CHARACTER THAT DOESN'T GET ENOUGH FAME...
IT'S BAD ENOUGH I'M GETTING INSULTED BY THE TROLL, ALRIGHT?

IT WASN'T ME, MONICA.
YOU CAN SEARCH MY HOUSE, MY COMPUTER, WHATEVER!

OF COURSE, I LIKED GETTING SOME ATTENTION...
... BUT IN THE END, IT ACTUALLY ENDED UP HURTING ME.
I COULDN'T EVEN FIND A LAB PARTNER, I FAILED A PROJECT.
Group project:
Sunny and Himself
F-

UGH! HE'S GOT A POINT!
THE KING OF TROLLS **CAN'T** BE SUNNY!

I DON'T KNOW WHAT TO DO ANYMORE! I'VE RUN OUT OF SUSPECTS!
I'VE INVESTI-GATED ALL THE ONES THAT...

... I KNOW?

THE KING OF TROLLS ONLY ATTACKS PEOPLE IN THE NEIGHBOR-HOOD!
BUT I DON'T KNOW THAT GUY! WHO COULD IT BE?

THE GUY IN THAT KISSING PHOTO!
WHO WAS HE?

WHY WOULD HE INVOLVE A STRANGER NOW?

WELL, IF IT ISN'T THE **HEART-BREAKER**!

LEAVE ME ALONE, TONY!
I'M NOT IN THE MOOD TODAY!

FINE, NO STRESS! I THOUGHT IT WAS KIND OF COOL HOW YOU FOOLED J-FIVE, IS ALL.
I **DIDN'T DO THAT**! THAT PHOTO WAS A FAKE!

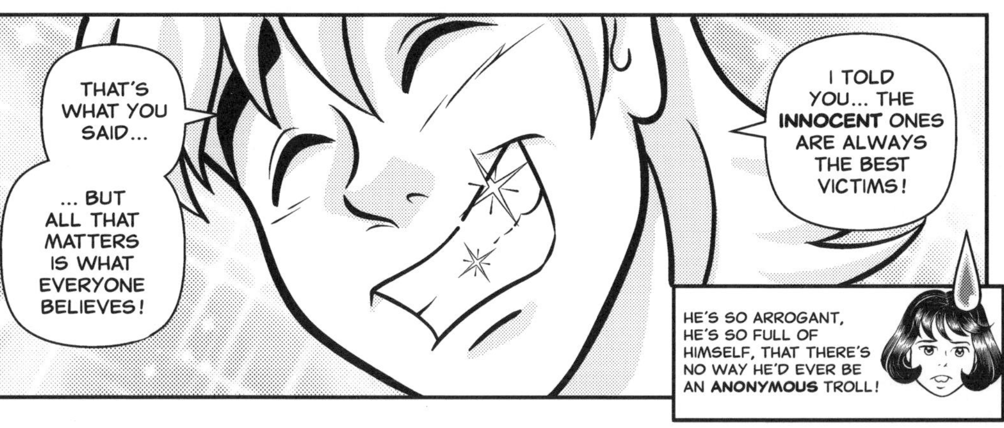
THAT'S WHAT YOU SAID...
... BUT ALL THAT MATTERS IS WHAT EVERYONE BELIEVES!
I TOLD YOU... THE **INNOCENT** ONES ARE ALWAYS THE BEST VICTIMS!
HE'S SO ARROGANT, HE'S SO FULL OF HIMSELF, THAT THERE'S NO WAY HE'D EVER BE AN **ANONYMOUS** TROLL!

AND YOU KNOW WHAT ELSE? IF YOU WERE GOING TO KISS SOMEONE TO HURT J...
... YOU SHOULD HAVE AT LEAST DONE IT WITH ME...

... INSTEAD OF THAT LOSER IN THE PICTURE!
YEAH, RIGHT, ME AND YOU... WE WOULD NEVER...

WAIT! HOLD UP!
TONY! YOU KNOW WHO THAT GUY IN THE PHOTO IS?!

ARE YOU KIDDING ME?
THE OTHER PEOPLE MIGHT HAVE FORGOTTEN HIM...

... BUT **YOU?!**

"WE EVEN LIVED ON THE SAME STREET!"
OH, MY GOODNESS... HOW LONG HAS IT BEEN SINCE I'VE BEEN HERE?
IT FEELS LIKE IT WAS A DECADE AGO!

HELLO? HOW MAY I HELP YOU?

IT REALLY IS YOU! THAT APPEARANCE, IT CAN ONLY BE YOU!
... IT'S BEEN A LONG TIME SINCE WE'VE TALKED...

...FANTASTIC FREDDIE!
HA-HA! THAT'S ME!
I FORGOT ALL ABOUT THAT RIDICULOUS NICKNAME FROM WHEN WE WERE YOUNGER!

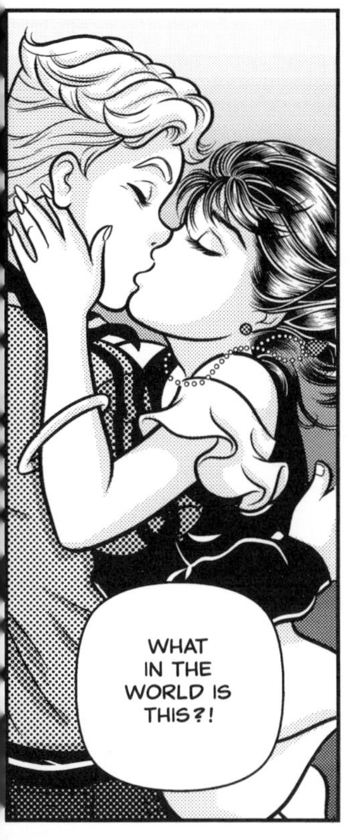
WHAT IN THE WORLD IS THIS?!

THIS IS ABSURD! WHAT WILL MY GIRLFRIEND SAY ABOUT THIS?
THE SAME THAT THING THAT J-FIVE SAID.
THE KING OF TROLLS IS GOING AROUND SPREADING GOSSIP ABOUT EVERYONE.

EVIL GOSSIP, BLOWN OUT OF PROPORTION, BUT ALWAYS **TRUE**.
THE ONLY TIME HE'S EVER LIED...

...WAS ABOUT ME AND YOU!

WELL, A LOT OF GUYS AROUND HERE REALLY DON'T LIKE ME.
IT'S NOT NECESSARILY EASY BEING POPULAR WITH THE LADIES!
WOW, HAHA, HOW **MODEST**!

YEAH, THE TROLL MUST HAVE USED YOUR PHOTO FOR THAT EXACT REASON!

I'VE NEVER SEEN THE **SITE**...
... BUT THE AUTHOR MUST HAVE SOME KIND OF **PERSONAL REASON**.
SOMEONE MAD AT THE BOTH OF US.

I JUST DON'T KNOW WHO IT POSSIBLY COULD BE BECAUSE...

... WELL, ***I KNOW***!

SORRY, MONICA! IT MIGHT NOT BE EASY FOR YOU TO HEAR...
... BUT I HAVE TO ASK YOU SOMETHING NONETHELESS.

YOU SAID THAT YOU SAW JIMMY WITH IRENE RIGHT **AFTER** THE PHOTO WAS POSTED?
YES!

AND HE WAS **NEVER** A VICTIM OF THE KING OF TROLLS, RIGHT?

HE'S **NEVER** APPEARED ON THE TROLL CASTLE, RIGHT?

N-NO...

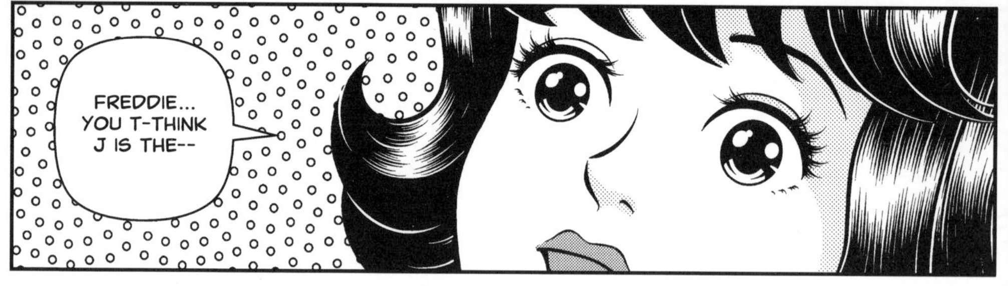
FREDDIE... YOU T-THINK J IS THE--

HE'S TRYING TO FIND A WAY OUT FROM YOU...
... AND THIS IS THE EXCUSE HE COMES UP WITH TO GET SOME SPACE BETWEEN YOU?

A WHOLE PLAN JUST TO MAKE IT SEEM LIKE IT'S *YOUR* FAULT?

I H-HADN'T THOUGHT OF THAT!
I THOUGHT HE WAS HIDING SOMETHING, BUT...

SO, THIS WHOLE TIME, HE JUST WANTED TO BE WITH IRENE?!

IF J-FIVE IS ANYTHING LIKE I RE-MEMBER...
...HE'S ALWAYS HAS **A PLAN** UP HIS SLEEVE!

B-BUT... W-WHAT ABOUT ALL THE PEOPLE HE'S UPSET?
J WOULD NEVER DO THAT TO HIS FRIENDS, HE'D...

ARE YOU **SURE** ABOUT THAT? FROM WHAT I REMEMBER...

... HE'S NEVER WORRIED TOO MUCH ABOUT INVOLVING HIS **FRIENDS** IN HIS PLANS.
EVEN WHEN THAT MEANT IT WOULDN'T TURN OUT SO GREAT FOR THEM.
THAT'S TRUE! I'M LIVING PROOF!

BESIDES, EVERYONE EXPECTS THE KING OF TROLLS TO BE UGLY AND JEALOUS!
THAT KEEPS EYES OFF HIM!
NO... IT CAN'T BE...
J-FIVE... THE KING OF TROLLS...

ALL OF IT, AN ELABORATE PLAN TO GET RID OF ME...

IT'S OKAY, MONICA! YOU AREN'T ALONE!

HE ATTACKED ME AS WELL.
LET'S DO THIS TOGETHER! LET'S SHOW PEOPLE WHAT HE'S REALLY DOING.

FREDDIE... THANK YOU.

MAYBE THIS HAS ALL BEEN DESTINY AT WORK, MONICA!

MAYBE THIS HAS WORKED TO BRING THE TWO OF US TOGETHER!

FREDDIE...?

YOU DESERVE BETTER THAN HIM.
SOMEONE SINCERE. SOMEONE WHO'S CONFIDENT.
I DON'T KNOW... I...

J-FIVE MIGHT THINK HE CAME OUT ON TOP, TRADING IN A BRUNETTE FOR A BLONDE...

... BUT IN THE END, HE'S DONE NOTHING MORE THAN HELP US BE TOGETHER.
HOW DID YOU KNOW?

WHAT?

HOW DID YOU KNOW THAT IRENE IS BLOND?

HUH... YOU MUST HAVE SAID SOMETHING AND--
I DIDN'T SAY A WORD!

WE ONLY MET IRENE IN **HIGH SCHOOL**!
AND BY THEN YOU WEREN'T AROUND ANYMORE!

I DON'T KNOW... I MEAN... I KNEW SOMEHOW... IT...

AND THERE'S MORE!
IF YOU DIDN'T KNOW ANYTHING ABOUT TROLL CASTLE...

... THEN HOW COULD YOU POSSIBLY KNOW J-FIVE HAS NEVER BEEN A VICTIM?!

OUT OF MY WAY! I'M COMING THROUGH!
HEY! YOU CAN'T JUST INVADE MY HOME LIKE THIS!

NO! THAT'S MY ROOM!
YOU CAN'T GO IN THERE!

I KNEW IT!

YOU ARE THE KING OF TROLLS!

AT LEAST YOU WERE RIGHT ABOUT ONE THING.
EVERYONE EXPECTS THE KING OF TROLLS TO BE UGLY AND JEALOUS.
THAT TAKES THE SUSPICION RIGHT OFF J-FIVE!

...BUT IT ALSO TAKES THE SUSPICION OFF OF **YOU**, WHICH...
FREDDIE!

OH, I'LL GET THAT...

HMM...

HUFF! PUFF!... POLICE! I'M CALLING THE POLICE!

I'LL SAY THAT SHE BROKE INTO MY HOUSE!
THEN, I'LL GET RID OF ALL OF THE EVIDENCE!
I'LL ERASE EVERYTHING FROM MY COMPUTER, AND...

GET BACK HERE, FREDDIE! IF YOU DON'T I'LL...

YOU'LL WHAT?!
NO PLUSH RABBIT TO HELP YOU OUT OF THIS ONE, HUH?

POF

TRUE! THERE ARE SOME TIMES THAT SAMSON COULD COME IN HANDY.
BUT AT LEAST THIS TIME...

... A TROLL WORKED JUST AS WELL!
OMG, DID SHE JUST TROLL ME?!

WHY, FREDDIE? *WHY* WOULD YOU DO THIS?!
WE HAVEN'T SEEN EACH OTHER IN *AGES*!

THAT'S EXACTLY WHY, YOU **SNOB**!

"SNOB"? ME?!

A SNOB AND CONCEITED! ***BOSS OF THE FLOCK***!
PEOPLE ALWAYS GOING OUT OF THEIR WAY TO FLATTER YOU.

VERY DIFFERENT THAN BACK IN THE DAY...

...WHEN YOU WERE **SHORT**, **BRATTY**, AND **CHUBBY**!
IN THOSE DAYS, YOU WERE CRAZY ABOUT ME.
TO YOU AND ALL THE OTHER GIRLS, I WAS THE NEIGHBORHOOD **HEARTTHROB**.

THEN CAME THE WHOLE "GROWING UP CHANGES PEOPLE" STORY.

AND EVERYONE FORGOT ABOUT ME!

NO ONE NOTICED WHEN I CHANGED SCHOOLS!
EVERYONE WAS TOO BUSY BEING THE **COOL KIDS**...

... AND EVERYONE LEFT ME BEHIND.

SO, I DECIDED TO REVEAL THE TRUTH.
TO SHOW ALL OF YOU THAT YOU DON'T KNOW EACH OTHER AS WELL AS YOU THINK YOU DO.

YOU'RE JUST SELFISH!
YOU ACTED LIKE YOU WERE SUPPORTING ME JUST TO TURN ME AGAINST J-FIVE!
OF COURSE! THAT RIDICULOUS BALD-BOY **STOLE MY PLACE** IN THE GROUP!
IF I COULD GET HIM TO BE **UNMASKED** AS THE KING OF TROLLS...

... THEN EVERYONE WOULD HATE HIM!
I'D GO BACK TO BEING MR. POPULAR!

BWA-HA-HA!

HA-HA-HA-HA!
WHAT'S SO FUNNY?!

YOU'RE SOOO CUTE!
YOU COULD HAVE COME BACK... MADE FRIENDS WITH EVERYONE...

... BUT INSTEAD YOU TROLL EVERYONE TO TRY AND SEEM LIKE THE GOOD GUY!

YOU ARE **SO** INSECURE AND RIDICULOUS... SO PETTY...

... THAT YOU CHOSE TO TRY AND **PUT EVERYONE DOWN** SO THAT YOU COULD MAKE YOURSELF SUPERIOR!
JUST FOR SOME **ATTENTION**!

NOT EVEN SUNNY WOULD ACT THIS WAY, SO NEEDY AND PATHETIC!
THANKS! *I THINK...?*

BUT I'VE HAD ENOUGH. YOUR STUPID ANTICS ARE OVER.
YOU'RE GOING TO HAVE TO FIND SOME OTHER WAY TO DEAL WITH ALL OF YOUR JEALOUSY.
OH, YEAH? AND HOW DO YOU INTEND TO STOP ME?
WITH YOUR PLUSH RABBIT?!

I'M NOT GOING TO STOP A THING.
YOU ARE GOING TO!

JUST LIKE MR. RUBENS SAID TO MAGGY...
FOLLOWING, HARASSING, AND SPYING ON PEOPLE IS **ILLEGAL**!
SPREADING LIES ABOUT SOMEONE IS **ALSO ILLEGAL**!

YOUR ENTIRE ***BLOG*** IS PROOF OF A CYBER CRIME!

B-BUT... IT WAS ALL JUST A JOKE!
I'M JUST A KID, I CAN'T BE CHARGED FOR A CRIME!

MAYBE! BUT YOUR PARENTS, WHO ARE RESPONSIBLE FOR YOU... CAN!
SO, IF YOU KNOW WHAT'S BEST FOR THEM...

... THE KING OF TROLLS IS ABOUT TO DISAPPEAR.
BUT, HEY! LOOK ON THE BRIGHT SIDE, YOU WANTED THE GANG'S **ATTENTION**...

"...AND YOU'RE ABOUT TO **GET IT**!"

SERIOUSLY? FANTASTIC FREDDIE?!
WEIIIRD! I HAVEN'T THOUGHT OF HIM IN YEARS!
SEEMS LIKE ***THAT*** WAS HIS PROBLEM.
WHO KNEW...?

EXACTLY AS I SUSPECTED!
SOME JEALOUS PERSON THAT THOUGHT WE WERE THE MOST IMPORTANT THING IN THEIR WORLD.
OKAY, MAN! ***I'M*** THE ONE THAT CAME UP WITH THAT!

YOU THINK YOU'RE SO SMART...
... BUT YOU FELL RIGHT INTO HIS TRAP!
GULP! BUT... BUT...
BUT THAT FAKE PHOTO WAS VERY **WELL DONE**!

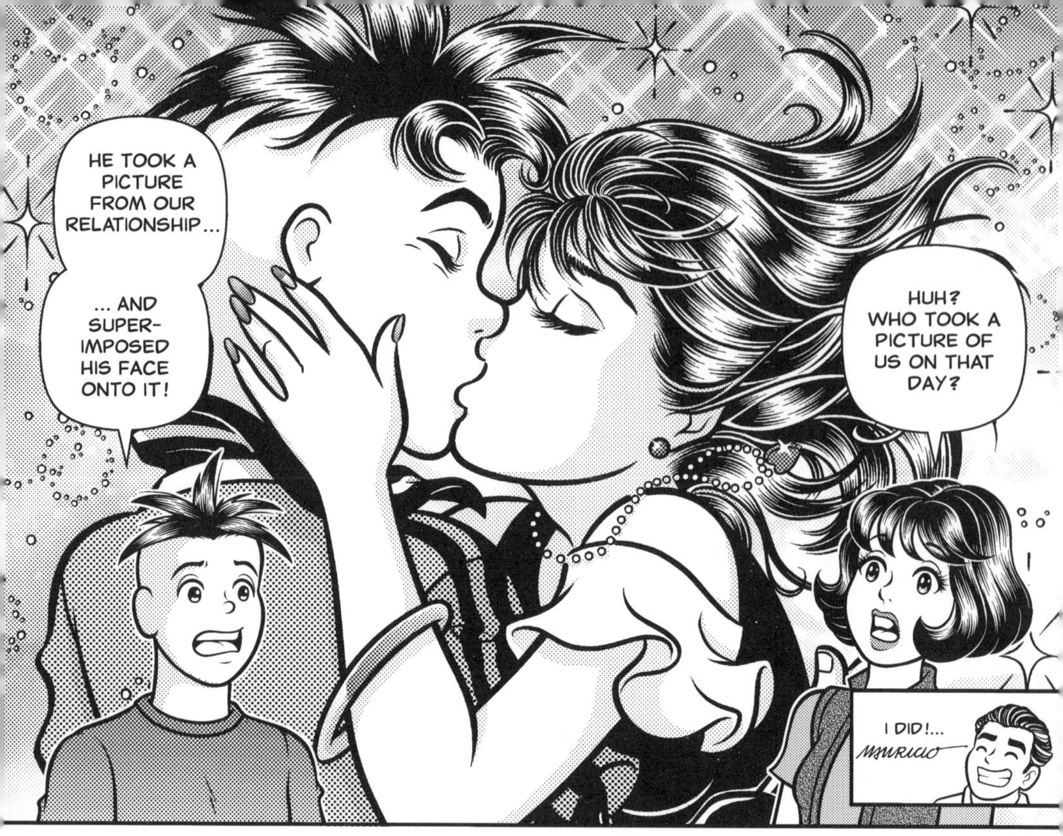
HE TOOK A PICTURE FROM OUR RELATIONSHIP...
... AND SUPER-IMPOSED HIS FACE ONTO IT!
HUH? WHO TOOK A PICTURE OF US ON THAT DAY?
I DID!...
MAURICIO

STILL, I SHOULD HAVE BELIEVED YOU. I'M SORRY.
IT'S FINE! I'M GUILTY OF THINKING YOU WERE HIDING SOMETHING TOO.

WE NEED TO **TRUST** EACH OTHER MORE.

SO, I CAN KEEP BEING FRIENDS WITH IRENE?
DON'T YOU PUSH IT, MISTER!

I'M SO GLAD! NO ONE BELIEVES THE EXAGGERATIONS AND LIES FROM THAT SITE.
MR. RUBENS IS GOING TO GO BACK TO BEING NICE TO ME!
SOME PEOPLE NEVER LEARN...

PSH! WELL, I FOR ONE, REALLY ENJOYED PEOPLE AROUND HERE GETTING TROLLED!

WELL, TONY... IT LOOKS LIKE THE TROLL CASTLE DID HAVE ONE LAST POST.
HUH?! YOU HAVE ACCESS TO IT HERE ON CAMPUS?

YES! I TOOK THE BAN OFF THE SITE WHEN I REALIZED IT WAS ALL EXAGGERATED.
I TOLD YOU SHE WAS MY COUSIN!

LET'S DO THIS! LET ME CHECK OUT THE LAST EPIC "DISH" FROM THE TROLL!

Two Ton Tony Falls Hard.
Helps Monica Against the King of Trolls!
Bad Boy or Push Over?
ARGH! I'M GLAD THIS THING IS GOING OFFLINE!
THAT JEALOUS HAS-BEEN JUST TRIED TO RUIN MY TOUGH GUY IMAGE!
THAT'S RIGHT, TONY! NOT EVEN YOU WERE SAFE FROM THE TROLL!
END

A SPECIAL MESSAGE FROM

MAURICIO DE SOUSA

THE CREATOR OF MONICA

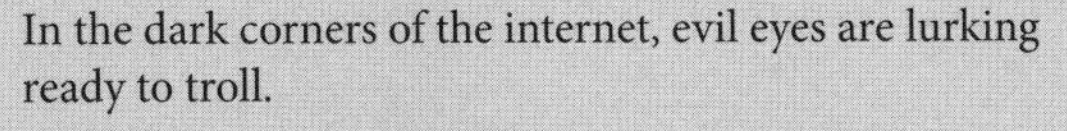

In the dark corners of the internet, evil eyes are lurking ready to troll.

And trolls can emerge where you least expect it.

Enemies of reason and peace, determined to create confusion, spread discord, and diminish self-confidence… this new villain should be called out and confronted.

But this is not a common fight, as we are acustomed to. This fight starts with our strategic escape. Because, at the first sign of an ounce of indifference, the Troll's power is diminished, the Troll dies. The Troll loses power when they aren't confronted or responded to. We don't always have the patience or energy to ignore the tricks of a troll. We are not always immune to our own weakness of wanting to speak out against trolling. But time shows that we are the ones losing when we confront them. Trolls lack ethics, morals, and limits. They are amoral.

If we enter on the same playing field as the trolls, we lower our standards, and end up pawns in their own game. Avoid this. Soften your reactions.

Walk away. It isn't cowardly; it's bold.

Contradicting your natural defense mechanisms demonstrates courage, force, and resolution. It helps "control" the beast.

Push it to the deep dark depths of the Internet.

Mauricio

Mauricio de Sousa

This story was originally published a few years ago in Brazil. Since then, cyberbullying has grown more prominent and actions have been taken to crackdown on trolls and protect children and teens who use the internet.
For more information on laws and to find help in your area, visit www.stopbullying.gov

Welcome to MONICA ADVENTURES #3 “Who's Saying Nasty Things About Me… Online?!” from those social media savvy types at Charmz, the Papercutz imprint devoted to romantic and fun graphic novels.

Back in MONICA ADVENTURES #1, we talked about Monica and her creator, Mauricio de Sousa. We explained that the character of Moncia started as a young girl taking charge of her neighborhood along with her friends (and frenemies) Maggy, Smudge, and "Jimmy" J-Five.

In this graphic novel series, Monica is a teenager in high school, it seems that not everyone she knew when she was younger may have grown up at the same speed intellectually. When we grow up, sometimes we lose touch with old classmates and people who might go to different schools. Do you have any old friends you may have lost touch with? While this volume focuses on the dangers (or entertainment if you ask Denise) of social media, and care should be taken online to protect your privacy, one of the great things about social media is the ability to re-connect with old friends. We feel that same way when enjoying a comic or graphic novel, even thought we realize these are ficticious characters, we still feel like we are connecting with dear old friends.

Monica is willing to break the internet to keep her friends happy and safe. She is a powerful friend not just in strength, but in her determination to problem solve and figure out the true identity of the Troll King who is causing all her friends harm. Heroic, everyday stories like these are the most relatable. Other strong protagonists in our Charmz line are just as heroic in their own way. Middle schooler Chloe Blin needs to stand up to bullies and face her fears as she starts a stressful internship in CHLOE #1. Amy Von Brandt, who goes to a private school, must cope as her mom is ready to date after the death of her father. AMY'S DIARY #1 is full of drama, as well as her trying to find her place in the world, if she even belongs to this world—the jury is still out on that. And then there's Cherry Costello who has to put on a brave face to face her four new step-sisters, not all of them happy to have her, as she and her chocolatier dad move-in in SWEETIES #1. Lastly, Crimson Volania Mulch has to piece herself together, literally, as she wakes up as a patchwork girl in a cemetary in STITCHED #1 . All of these young people have their own challenges to brave and their own important support systems in place made up of friends, family, and even teachers, coaches, or supervisors.

So, yes, all of these characters are fictional, but that doesn't mean we can't learn from them, does it?

STAY IN TOUCH!

EMAIL:	whitman@papercutz.com
WEB:	Papercutz.com
TWITTER:	@papercutzgn
INSTAGRAM:	@papercutzgn
FACEBOOK:	PAPERCUTZGRAPHICNOVELS
FANMAIL:	Charmz, 160 Broadway, Suite 700, East Wing, New York, NY 10038

MORE GRAPHIC NOVELS AVAILABLE FROM charmz™

STITCHED #1 "THE FIRST DAY OF THE REST OF HER LIFE"

STITCHED #2 "LOVE IN THE TIME OF ASSUMPTION"

G.F.F.s #1 "MY HEART LIES IN THE 90s"

G.F.F.s #2 "WITCHES GET THINGS DONE"

ANA AND THE COSMIC RACE #1 "THE RACE BEGINS"

CHLOE #1 "THE NEW GIRL"

CHLOE #2 "THE QUEEN OF HIGH SCHOOL"

CHLOE #3 "FRENEMIES"

CHLOE #4 "RAINY DAY"

CHLOE #5 "CARNIVAL PARTY"

SCARLET ROSE #1

SCARLET ROSE #2

SCARLET ROSE #3

SCARLET ROSE #4

SCARLET ROSE #5

MONICA ADVENTURES #1

MONICA ADVENTURES #2

MONICA ADVENTURES #3

MONICA ADVENTURES #4

MONICA ADVENTURES #5

AMY'S DIARY #1

AMY'S DIARY #2

AMY'S DIARY #3

SWEETIES #1

SWEETIES #2

SEE MORE AT PAPERCUTZ.COM

NOOOOOOOPE...
You got it all backwards! You can't read this comic if you start from here. I understand that the original Japanese manga is read in the traditional "right to left" style... But I had a little conversation with Mauricio and he let us keep our stories the way we are accustomed to - from left to right. Let's agree that even though these comics have a manga style that we respect very much, there is still much of the original Monica's Gang in them too...
Enjoy!
Monica.
"IT ALL STARTED TODAY AFTER CLASS..."
HA-HA! HA-HA!
AW "J", YOU ARE SO ADORABLE!
WHAT?
GULP! UM... I SAID "THAT LAST ONE WAS HORRIBLE"!
I HAVE TO GO!
GOOD THINGS OR BAD?
REALLY?!
ALRIGHTY!

AFTER ALL, YOU'VE YET TO HAVE YOUR TURN AT THE *TROLL CASTLE*.